This book belongs to

_____

Deep Snow

Deep Snow

by Robert Munsch

illustrated by Michael Martchenko

Scholastic Canada Ltd.
Toronto New York London Auckland Sydney
Mexico City New Delhi Hong Kong Buenos Aires

Scholastic Canada Ltd.
604 King Street West, Toronto, Ontario M5V 1E1, Canada

Scholastic Inc.
557 Broadway, New York, NY 10012, USA

Scholastic Australia Pty Limited
PO Box 579, Gosford, NSW 2250, Australia

Scholastic New Zealand Limited
Private Bag 94407, Botany, Manukau 2163, New Zealand

Scholastic Children's Books
Euston House, 24 Eversholt Street, London NW1 1DB, UK

www.scholastic.ca

The art for this book was painted in watercolour on Crescent illustration board.
The type is set in 24 point Perpetua Regular.

Library and Archives Canada Cataloguing in Publication

Munsch, Robert N., 1945-, author
Deep snow / by Robert Munsch ; illustrated by Michael Martchenko.

ISBN 978-1-4431-7058-1 (softcover)

I. Martchenko, Michael, illustrator II. Title.

PS8576.U575D44 2019   jC813'.54   C2018-904218-4

6 5 4 3 2 1   Printed in Malaysia 108   19 20 21 22 23

To Ali and Kate Lucas,
Goose Bay, Newfoundland and Labrador.
— R.M.

Way out in the middle of nowhere, Ali suddenly yelled, "STOP!"

"What's the matter?" said her father.

"I want to jump in the snow," said Ali.

"No," said her sister Kate, "that is deep, deep, deeeeeeep snow!"

"I still want to jump in it," said Ali.

"This is not a good idea," said Kate.

Ali stood up on the seat, gave her best yell, jumped out as far as she could, landed in the snow and disappeared:

WHOOMPH!

All that was left was a hole in the snow.

"She is totally gone," said Kate. "She's at the bottom of a drift."

"Kate," said their father, "jump down that hole and help Ali get out."

"This is also a bad idea," said Kate, but she jumped down the hole anyway:

WHOOMPH!

For a long time nothing happened.

Then their father climbed off the snowmobile, crawled over to the hole in the snow and said, "Hey, Ali and Kate! How are you doing down there?"

Ali and Kate said, "Murf bluk bwaaaaaah," because their mouths were full of snow.

Their father said, "Ali and Kate, speak clearly. I can't hear you."

Ali got the snow out of her mouth and yelled, "GET US OUT OF HERE!"

"Don't worry," said their father. He reached down the hole as far as he could, got hold of something and pulled very hard.

Ali yelled, "AAAAHHHHHH! That's my ear!"

So he let go of Ali's ear, reached down the hole, got hold of something else and pulled very hard.

Kate yelled, "AAAAHHHHHH! That's my nose!"

So he let go of Kate's nose, reached down the hole as far as he could, got hold of something else and pulled very hard.

Ali yelled, "AAAAHHHHHH! That's my lip!"

Finally their dad got hold of their ponytails and pulled as hard as he could, and Ali and Kate came flying out of the hole.

"Good," said their dad. "Now we can go."

"No, we can't," said Ali and Kate. "Our boots are still at the bottom of the hole."

"Oh, rats," said their father. He crawled over to the hole and reached down as far as he could. He didn't find their boots, so he reached way, way, way, WAY down and fell into the hole:

WHOOMPH!

Only his boots were sticking up out of the snow.

Ali crawled over to the boots and said, "Hey, Dad! How are you doing down there?"

Their father said, "Murf bluk bwaaaaaah," because his mouth was full of snow.

"Speak clearly," said Kate. "We can't understand you."

"Murf bluk bwaaaaaah," said their father, and then he got the snow out of his mouth and yelled, "GET ME OUT OF HERE!"

Ali and Kate took hold of their dad's feet and pulled as hard as they could. Nothing happened.

"This is very bad," said Ali. "Daddy will have to stay there till springtime. How can he fly his jet if he is stuck at the bottom of a hole?"

Then Kate got an idea. She ran over to the snowmobile and got a rope. She tied one end of the rope around their father's foot and tied the other end to the snowmobile. Then Ali and Kate jumped on the snowmobile and went down the trail as fast as they could:

VROOOOMM!

Their father came flying up out of the hole and bounced down the trail after the snowmobile yelling:

"Ow ouch! Ow ouch! Ow ouch! STOP! STOP! STOP! STOP!"

So Kate stopped the snowmobile and there was their father, lying in the snow.

"Daddy," said Ali, "you didn't get our boots after all. We're going to have to do it again."

"Right," said their father. "Let's do it again."

He tied a rope to Ali and Kate's feet and dropped them down the hole.

About Deep Snow

In 1991, I was on a storytelling trip in Labrador. My son, Andrew, was with me. In Goose Bay we stayed with Ali and Kate Lucas, whose dad was a Canadian Forces pilot. Andrew liked jet planes, and I thought, "Wow! I bet I am going to get a good jet plane story."

One afternoon we went for a walk on a snowmobile trail. Andrew and I did not know that the snow in the woods was very, very deep. Andrew thought it would be fun to jump off the trail, and he went way down into the snow. He loved it. Ali and Kate jumped in after him.

They did not go that far down into the snow, but Kate got her foot stuck, so I went to help. I did not know that in some places the snow was covering

whole pine trees and the trees made an empty place under the snow. So when I walked off the trail I fell through, way, way, way over my head.

It took me a long time to climb back up, and Kate was still stuck! We finally got her out, but her boots were still at the bottom of the hole. Since I was already wet, I went head-first down into the hole to get her boots.

While I was head-first in the snow with my feet sticking out, I started thinking of a story called "Deep Snow." So this is my only story that started while I was upside-down in the snow.

Me and Andrew (on the snowmobile) near Goose Bay, Labrador. On this trip we also met Cheryl Allen, standing on the left, and I wrote the story *Give Me Back My Dad!* for her.

If you liked Deep Snow, try these other great books by Robert Munsch!

ISBN 978-1-4431-0764-8

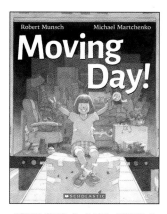

ISBN 978-1-4431-6399-6

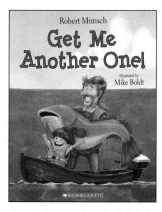

ISBN 978-1-4431-6328-6

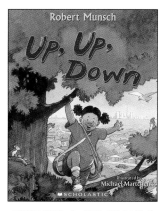

ISBN 978-0-439-98815-5

ISBN 978-1-4431-4617-3

ISBN 978-1-4431-1318-2

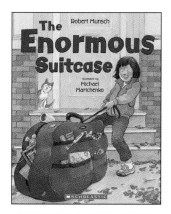

ISBN 978-1-4431-6318-7

ISBN 978-1-4431-4290-8

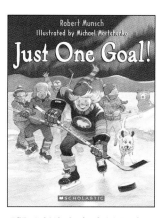

ISBN 978-0-545-99035-6

Visit www.scholastic.ca/munsch for more information about Robert Munsch and his books, along with games, activities, a printable checklist and more!